# TEENAGE MUTANT NINJA TURTLES

## COMIC BOOK HEROES

adapted by Jim Thomas
based on the original teleplay by Marty Isenberg
illustrated by Aristides Ruiz and Mike Giles

Ready-to-Read

Simon Spotlight
New York   London   Toronto   Sydney

Based on the TV series *Teenage Mutant Ninja Turtles*™
as seen on Fox and Cartoon Network®

SIMON SPOTLIGHT
An imprint of Simon & Schuster Children's Publishing Division
1230 Avenue of the Americas, New York, New York 10020
© 2005 Mirage Studios, Inc. *Teenage Mutant Ninja Turtles*™ is a trademark of
Mirage Studios, Inc. All rights reserved.
SIMON SPOTLIGHT, READY-TO-READ, and colophon are registered
trademarks of Simon & Schuster, Inc.
All rights reserved, including the right of reproduction in whole
or in part in any form.
Manufactured in the United States of America
First Edition
2 4 6 8 10 9 7 5 3 1
Library of Congress Cataloging-in-Publication Data
Thomas, Jim K., 1970-
Comic book heroes / adapted by Jim Thomas ; based on the original teleplay by
Marty Isenberg ; illustrated by Art Ruiz and Mike Giles.– 1st ed.
p. cm. – (Ready-to-read)
"Based on the TV series Teenage Mutant Ninja Turtles(tm) as seen on
Fox and Cartoon Network(tm)."
Summary: When Michelangelo discovers his favorite comic book heroes are real, he he
them combat the enemy, using an idea from one of their past adventures.
ISBN 1-4169-0074-8
[1. Turtles–Fiction. 2. Heroes–Fiction. 3. Martial arts–Fiction. 4. Cartoons and
comics–Fiction.] I. Isenberg, Marty. II. Ruiz, Art, ill. III. Giles, Mike, ill. IV. Teenage
Mutant Ninja Turtles (Television program : 2003- ) V. Title. VI. Series.
PZ7.T3669544Com 2005
[E]–dc22
2004027824

# HAPTER ONE

Michelangelo read his comic book.
General Mayhem's Robo Tanks
e no match for Stainless Steve Steel,
octor Dome, Battling Bernice, Zippy Lad,
ey Lastic, and Metal Head . . . the
stice Force!'"

Michelangelo quickly turned the page. "'Stainless Steve only ever sees me as his teammate, Battling Bernice,'" he read. "'But we could be so much more. And even though Doctor Dome still has feelings for me, he would never forgive me if he knew my secret.'"

Michelangelo flipped another page and suddenly yelled, "'To be continued?'"

He searched through his pile of comic books. "I *have* to know if Battling Bernice survived! And did she end up with Stainless Steve or Doctor Dome?"

"Michelangelo!" called Master Splinter. "As you see, I'm trying to meditate. To quiet and calm my spirit. Note the words 'quiet' and 'calm.'"

Michelangelo nodded. "Yes, Master," he said. Then he started calling comic book stores.

Just then the elevator doors opened and Casey Jones walked in. His boom box was blasting heavy metal music.

Shaking his head, Splinter turned off Casey's boom box with his walking stick.

Michelangelo hung up the phone. "I can't believe it!" he said. "No one in this city has a copy of *Justice Force* number one thirty-seven!"

"You should try Steve's Comics," Casey said. "Of course he's all the way up in Northampton . . ."

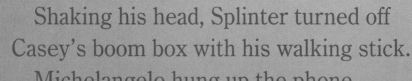

# CHAPTER TWO

When Casey and the Turtles got to Steve's Comics in Northampton, Michelangelo found the owner, Steve.

"I'm sorry, friend," Steve said. "There *is* no *Justice Force* number one thirty-seven."

"But I *have* to know what happened to Battling Bernice!" Michelangelo said.

Steve shook his head sadly. "She didn't make it," he said.

"How would you know?" asked Michelangelo.

But Steve was not looking at Michelangelo. He was staring at something behind the Turtle—at two robots with glowing domes on their heads!

"Domeoids!" Steve shouted.

Suddenly more Domeoids crashed into the store. Leonardo whipped out his katanas.

"This is a *working* vacation," he said.

Michelangelo was confused. "That's Metal Head. And you must be Stainless Steve! Then the Justice Force is real!"

Just then the Domeoids jetted off with Metal Head.

"Only Doctor Dome has the brain power to run all these Domeoids," Steve cried.

"But isn't Doctor Dome one of the good guys?" Michelangelo asked.

"Dome had always blamed us for Battling Bernice's death," said Steve. He took an old toggle switch out of his pocket and flipped the switch.

"That's the Justice Force emergency signal!" Michelangelo said.

The Turtles and Casey went back to Steve's home to decide what to do.

"I can't believe Doctor Dome would turn evil," Michelangelo said.

Steve shook his head. "You can't ignore the facts, Michelangelo."

Raphael laughed. "Michelangelo can ignore a lot of things!"

"Who's this old guy in a wheelchair?"
Casey asked.

"Watch who you're calling old, slowpoke!"
the man said.

"Hey, it's Zippy Lad!" Michelangelo said.
"And Joey Lastic!"

Suddenly Leonardo heard something and
looked up at the ceiling. "Guys!" he shouted.
"Something's on the roof!"

The Turtles and Casey hurried to the
roof—and found an army of Domeoids!
It didn't take long for the Turtles to
defeat them. But while they were
busy fighting them, several Domeoids
kidnapped the Justice Forcers.

"Oh, no!" Michelangelo said. "They've got
ippy Lad and Joey Lastic!"

"Not for long," Donatello said. "I planted
urtle Trackers on the old guys earlier.
ist in case."

Raphael crossed his arms. "Then what are
e waiting for?"

# CHAPTER THREE

The Turtles, Casey, and Steve followed the tracking signal through the forest, all the way to Doctor Dome's lab. But it was guarded by hundreds of Domeoids!

Steve studied them through binoculars.
"The Domeoids will attack anything that
doesn't give off the right signal," he said.

"Then we'll just have to get the right
signal," Donatello said, letting everyone in
on his idea.

"We look ridiculous," Raphael said.

"We'll look even worse getting beaten by a hundred Domeoids," said Donatello.

Wearing their new domes, the Turtles, Casey, and Stainless Steve walked right pas Doctor Dome's army of Domeoids.

Inside the lab the Turtles found several large domes filled with mist. Stainless Steve butted one of them. It cracked, and the mist leaked out. Inside was Metal Head!

Suddenly the wall exploded, and a huge Domebot burst through. Piloting the Domebot was Doctor Dome!

"Surrender, Steve!" Doctor Dome called. "You kidnapped the others, but you won't get me without a fight!"

"You accuse *me* of your twisted scheme?" Steve shouted. "This is *your* lab!"

With a mighty blow the Domebot broke open the other domes. Zippy Lad and Joey Lastic tumbled out.

"Admit your treachery," Doctor Dome cried, "or perhaps your captives will!"

"It's Doctor Dome!" Zippy yelled.
"Stop that traitor!"

"What?" Doctor Dome cried. "No!
Steve is the traitor!"

"Wait!" Michelangelo called. "Stop!
You both are friends, remember?"

# CHAPTER FOUR

Suddenly an army of Domeoids marched into the lab.

"Ah-ha!" Steve cried. "The Domeoids only glow like that when Doctor Dome is controlling them!"

"But if I were controlling them," Doctor Dome said, "my dome would be glowing too!"

Donatello was confused. "But if you're not controlling them, who is?"

"I am," said a voice.

The Domeoids stepped to the side as a woman walked toward Steve and Doctor Dome.

"Battling Bernice?" asked Doctor Dom

"How is that possible?" asked Stainless Steve.

"*Not* Battling Bernice," the woman said "I am her daughter, Ananda. You lured Bernice back into the Force and got her killed. Now I will have my revenge!"

Ananda nodded, and in an instant giant
rms grabbed the Justice Forcers—
d the Turtles and Casey as well!

Doctor Dome frowned. "How are you
le to control my robots?" he asked.

With an evil grin Ananda said,
thought you would have figured that out
now . . . Daddy!"

Ananda removed her helmet. Her head
as a clear dome, just like Doctor Dome's!

Doctor Dome was shocked, but he thought hard. "Must . . . try . . . to . . . gain . . . contr

Suddenly the Domebot and the arms let go of the Justice Force.

"Oh no, you don't!" Ananda cried. Her head glowed brightly as the Domebot, the Domeoids, and the arms attacked again.

Just then Michelangelo shouted,
"Everyone attack in different directions!
Split her focus!"

Ananda scowled. "Too much happening at
once!" she shouted.

Suddenly sparks and steam began flying
out of the Domeoids and the Domebot
overloaded.

"Nooo!" Ananda cried.

But it was too late. The Domebot and
Domeoids self-destructed.

Doctor Dome walked over to Ananda. "Look at me, daughter," he said. "Your mother chose to give her life to save others. But you still have one parent who's alive and wants to be part of your life."

# CHAPTER FIVE

"Michelangelo, how'd you come up with such a clever plan?" Joey Lastic asked.

Michelangelo smiled. "That's what *you* guys did in issue number fifty-seven!" he said.

"Michelangelo's geekdom finally pays off," Raphael said, laughing.

"Hey, Michelangelo," Steve said. He handed Michelangelo the Justice Force emergency signal switch. "Consider yourself an honorary member."